first experiences

Mummy's having a baby

This book belongs to...

· ·

first experiences

Mummy's having a baby

Written by Jillian Harker

Illustrated by Michelle White

Bright ☆ Sparks

Josh was helping his mum to do the washing-up.

"Guess what, Josh?" said Mum. "Soon, you're going to have a baby brother or sister to play with." She bent down and wiped some bubbles off his nose.

"Will the baby look like me?" asked Josh.

Mum laughed. "Oh, I hope so," she said. "Now, you'll have to help me. We've got *lots* to do before baby arrives."

The very next day,
Josh and his mum
went shopping.
They chose some
stripy baby-grows…

… a furry teddy bear
and a brand new car
seat – *all* for the baby!

"What about *me*?"
thought Josh.

Just then, Mum gave
Josh a present. "Here
you are," she said.
"Thanks for helping me."

"Thanks, Mum!" cried
Josh.

When they got home, Dad had brought Josh's old cot and buggy down from the attic.

Josh lay in the buggy and ate his tea.

"But what about *me*?" he said, sadly. "That's *my* cot."

"You don't need this anymore," laughed Dad. "You're a big boy now." Josh smiled.

As the weeks went by,
Josh waited… and
waited… and waited!

Was this baby
ever going to
arrive?

Then, one day, Mum said, "I'm going to the hospital, Josh. I think baby is coming today."

"But what about *me*?" asked Josh.

"Don't worry," said Mum. "Granny is here to look after you."

"I love Granny, but I don't want you to go," sniffed Josh. "I'll miss you."

"I'll miss you, too," said Mum and she hugged him tightly. "Don't worry. I'll be back soon."

Later that day, Dad came home from the hospital.

"Josh!" he called. "You've got a beautiful baby sister. Come on, I'll take you to meet her. We've called her Molly."

When they got to the hospital…

… Dad took lots of photos – of baby Molly!

"What about *me*?" grumbled Josh, quietly. He was feeling left out.

Then, Dad said, "Let's have a picture of Josh and Molly together." He took the photo… then another… and another!

Josh felt much better.

When Mum and Molly came home, lots of friends came to visit.

They all wanted to see Josh's sister and they brought lots of presents — for the baby!

"What about *me*?" thought Josh.

"Look what Molly has bought for you," said Mum.

And there, in Molly's cot, was a big parcel, tied up with a bow.

"Thanks for my train," said Josh and he gave his sister a *big* kiss.

Little babies take a lot of looking after!
Molly always seemed to be hungry…

… and her nappy needed changing a lot! She liked being cuddled, too.

"What about *me*?" thought Josh. "Will someone cuddle me, please?"

When Dad came home, he scooped Josh up and cuddled him. "I need a hug, too," said Dad. "Who will give me one?"

"I will," squealed Josh, laughing.

When they walked in the park,
everyone wanted to look at baby Molly. No one
seemed to notice Josh... except Mrs Jackson.

"Molly looks just like you," she said.

Josh smiled, proudly. "I think her nose is like
mine," he said.

Mum was
getting tired.

"Looking after
Molly is very
hard work,"
said Dad.

"What about *me*?"
said Josh. "I can help Mum."

So, when Molly was upset, Josh pulled funny faces and made his sister laugh.

When Molly wanted to play, Josh built brick towers and let her knock them down, again… and again… and again!

And when Molly dropped her rattle, Josh *always* picked it up for her.

At the supermarket, Mum let Josh push the buggy, which made him very happy.

Everyone stopped to talk to him and his sister.

"You really *are* Mummy's little helper, aren't you, Josh?" they said.

And Josh was the only one who could get
Molly off to sleep. He sang all his favourite
songs to her.

With Josh's help, Mum had more time to spare.

"Who wants a story and a nice, big cuddle?"
she asked, sitting on the sofa.

"I do," laughed Josh.

Mum started to read a story.

Suddenly, Josh asked, "What about Molly? Can she hear the story, too?"

"Of course, she can," laughed Mum and went to fetch her. Then, Mum started to read again.

"What about *me*?" asked Dad, as he sat on the sofa. "Can I listen?"

"Of course, you can," laughed Josh. "Molly and I want *everyone* to join in."

This is a Bright Sparks Book
First published in 2002
BRIGHT SPARKS, Queen Street House,
4 Queen Street, Bath BA1 1HE, UK

Copyright © PARRAGON 2002

Created and produced by THE COMPLETE WORKS

ISBN 1-84250-541-6

Printed in China